# VIRILE

## WHISKEY RUN: SAVAGE INK

HOPE FORD

# 1

## GRACIE

THERE'S NOT REALLY a bad part of town in Whiskey Run, but there are parts of town that my father has forbidden me from going to. The Distillery is one of them. But that's never really bothered me. I have no reason to go there. I'm not old enough to drink so what would be the point? But the other places I've been forbidden to go are on the other side of town around the Whiskey Whistler Bar. There are a bunch of businesses—a pawn shop, a liquor store, a tattoo shop, a bar—and my father has instilled in my brain that I have no reason to be "on that side" of town. And I've listened to him. I always listen to him. I always do exactly what I'm told. But not today.

I turned eighteen today. I've had all these dreams for when this day would come. I would finally be

1

free. I could live my life the way I want to instead of how my dad told me I needed to. I've done everything he's asked of me. I graduated with a four point five. I was valedictorian. I joined the clubs he wanted me to join. Hell, I hated French club, but I joined it because that's what he wanted me to do. I never bucked him because even though he's my father, I also know he's an evil man. When my mother died five years ago, he changed, and there's no reaching him now. He wants things his way or else you face the wrath of Brandon Franklin... also known as the mayor of Whiskey Run.

I take a deep breath as I walk down the cobbled sidewalk. I'm doing my best not to draw attention to myself, but I can feel all the eyes on me. Some of them probably know who I am, but most of them don't. My father has made sure I've stayed out of the limelight, and at least for that I'm thankful.

I reach into my purse and wrap my hand around the tiny sketchbook in there. That has been my freedom. When I wasn't allowed to do anything except school or school-sponsored events, I started drawing. My father didn't approve, and since the first time I showed him, when he ripped the drawing in two, I haven't shown him another piece of work.

But today... I have to do something. I have to.

I thought for sure when I turned eighteen I could do what I want. That's what I've been holding out for. I was accepted to the University of Berkeley all the way on the other side of the country. It's far... but I still worried it wouldn't be far enough. And then my father dropped his bombshell on me today. He had written the university and declined the full scholarship I had been offered. I called them to try and convince them to give me the scholarship back, but I was told that they had already offered it to someone else. In one afternoon, my dreams for my future were shattered. My father gave me the acceptance letter to Jasper College, the local community college where I would be able to stay at home and commute back and forth to school. In that instant, I wanted to die. I didn't want to spend one more day in his house with him.

I waited until he'd left for his weekly town meeting, stuffed my sketchbook into my purse, and walked out of the house. I know I need a way out, and I'm not giving up, but I need a plan. I'm not stupid enough to think I can leave without any money, plus I wouldn't get very far with the GPS tracker he has hidden on my car. So I walked to town, taking alleys and backstreets to get me to the other side of town. I don't stop until I'm outside Savage Ink.

The sign is yellow with black lettering that looks like graffiti. I lift my head and look at the big building in front of me. I'm not worried about changing my mind, because it's already been made up. I want this...no, I need this. This may be ridiculous to some, but to me it's going to be my very first taste of freedom.

·

---

## Aiden

I LOOK AROUND THE SHOP, and just like every other time I do, a sense of pride hits me in the chest. I worked hard to open this shop, and finally after five years, I have the building almost paid off and I've finally started to recognize my success. The days of living paycheck to paycheck are over. Of course I never had to really. My family has always been willing to help me out, and I have access to a big trust fund, but I've never wanted to use it. I wanted to do this all on my own terms. I'm now a sought-after tattoo artist, and I definitely don't take it for granted. My client that just left came all the way from Jasper to get his tattoo. Jasper isn't all that far away... just thirty to forty-five minutes, but there are three really well-known tattoo shops there, and I can't help but feel a little pride in knowing he came to me instead of just going down the street from his house.

I finish washing my hands when I hear the door ding out front. I sigh because I'm dog tired and ready to go home, maybe drink a shot of Blaze Whiskey, and head to bed. The walk from the back to the front, I remind myself to put another ad out for help. We are in desperate need of a receptionist. I have no appointments, and Treyton and Dawson have already left for the day, so it leaves me to deal with the unwanted newcomer.

"We're closed," I say before I even walk across the threshold from the back to the lobby area. I stop suddenly in my tracks and as soon as I realize my mouth is hanging open, I slam it shut.

The woman standing in front of me is not the usual type we get in here. She's an innocent. It's obvious by the way the cardigan is buttoned all the way up to her neck. She has mid-length blond hair with the prettiest pink lips I've ever seen. Instantly, images of exactly what those puffy lips could be doing has my dick hard and my heart racing.

Her eyes are taking me in, and I swear she's as stunned by me as I am by her. She takes a step backward. "I'm sorry. I didn't know you were closing."

She turns to leave, and my heart plummets. There's no way I can let her leave, not now when I don't even know her name. Fuck that, I may never let her leave.

I reach out to stop her, wrapping my hand around her arm. "Hold up. I'm not in any rush. What can I do for you?" I ask her plainly, but even I can hear the dirty thoughts that are making my voice almost growly.

I take a step toward her, my hand still on her, and I pull her to me almost possessively.

She turns her head but not her body, which is fine with me. I swear her ass is cradled right against my cock, and I don't want to lose that feeling. She lifts her eyes to me, and her voice is trembling. "A... tattoo. I came for a tattoo, but I didn't think... I should have made an appointment."

I should let her go, I know I should. I'm probably scaring the fuck out of her, but I can't force myself to open my hand and release her... not until I know she's not going to run.

"I can do your tattoo."

She blinks in confusion, as if she's trying to formulate what I just said to her. "But I thought you were closed."

I smirk, smiling at her as my hand moves up to the base of her neck. I'm taking way more liberties with her than I should, but she doesn't seem offended or put off by it. "I'd be a fool to let you leave without putting my mark on you."

2

GRACIE

HE'S SMILING AT ME. He's so close, I can smell his manly scent, and it's not any cologne or anything I've ever smelled before. I wonder if it's just him. Whatever it is, I want to take deep breaths, inhaling him in, and I wish that somehow, I could bottle it and smell it later when I'm alone in my room tonight.

I can feel my face heat at the thought. His hand tightens on my neck, and I bite my lip to hold in the whimper. There's a pull in my lower belly, and I can feel the moisture between my legs. All of this, everything that I'm feeling is new to me, and I don't have a clue what to think about it or do with it. I should probably be indignant. At the very least, I should put some distance between us, but I don't. I stand exactly where I'm at, my heart racing in my chest. "What do you mean put your mark on me?"

He's staring at me, and I stand here, biting my lip.

He lifts his hand, and I miss the strong pressure around my neck. That is until his thumb wipes across my lip so I'm not biting it anymore. I suck in a deep breath and hold it. The need to stick my tongue out and taste him is overpowering, and I swear he's waiting for it... maybe even hoping for it.

He searches my eyes. "A tattoo. I'm going to put a tattoo on you."

I let out a breath remembering why I'm here, and the day comes back at me like a Mack truck. I pull from his grasp. "Yes, I'd like a tattoo, but I can schedule an appointment."

He's angry... maybe not angry, but he's not happy that I pulled away. Well, I'm not either. I'm already imagining his hands on me and the feelings it will invoke on me. But my life is in shambles right now. I'm in no position to date... plus my father won't allow it.

He breaks through my thoughts. "Come to the back, you can go through the books and find what you want."

He turns away from me, and I have no choice but to follow him. I couldn't imagine walking away from him right now. He may be someone I just met and I don't know anything about him, but he's definitely the best thing to happen to me today. I'm not ready to just let it go yet.

I walk behind him, watching the way his back muscles stretch the Henley shirt across his shoulders. His jeans are snug, and I'm definitely appreciating his tight butt. I follow him down the hallway, and he walks into a room with a big sprawling chair, a counter with supplies and then two chairs up against the wall. He's watching me again. "This is a nice place, not what I expected." I cringe, did I just say that out loud? "I mean..."

He holds his hand up to stop me. "No, it's fine. I know what you meant. And thank you, this is my place. I'm Aiden Savage."

"Savage Ink," I mutter, making the connection with his last name and the name of the shop.

His lips curl up as he nods. He points to the chair, and I lift myself up onto the edge of it. "Tell me your name," he demands.

From anyone else it would sound bossy or rude, but from him all it does is make that pull in my lower belly tug even harder. I don't know what he's doing to me, but I know I like it. "Gracie," I tell him in a half whisper.

"Gracie," he repeats huskily. He looks me up and down, burning a path on my body. "That name suits you."

Before I can ask him what he means, he grabs a book off the counter. "These are the tattoos I've done before, but I'm thinking I'd like to do something unique for you."

I grab the book, because even though I know the design I want, I still want to see his work. I open the first page and am floored. "You did these?" I ask in awe.

He nods, and I swear there is a pink tinge on his cheeks like he's embarrassed. "They are amazing." I keep flipping through the book, and every tattoo is better than the last. "My goodness, Aiden, you really have talent."

He ignores my compliment. "Tell me what you were thinking, and we can start from there."

I set the book down on the chair beside me and reach into my purse. I'm almost embarrassed to pull the artwork out. I never let anyone see any of my drawings except for my dad that one time, and it seems even riskier now to have Aiden look at it. He's a professional artist. I would be devastated if he said he didn't like it.

I pull the small sketchbook out and flip to the last page. Taking a deep breath, I hand it to him and lower my eyes. I can't see his reaction. I don't want to.

The room is completely silent, but I still don't look at him. I bind my hands together in my lap and stare at the chipped polish on my thumb.

His voice is deep and fills the room. "Can I look at the rest of them?"

Finally, I look at him. "Why? That's the one I want."

He lifts the book up between us. "Because this is surreal, Gracie. It's beautiful and breathtaking... I swear it looks as if it could fly right off the page. You're gifted." He grips the book tighter. "Please, let me look."

I let out the breath I've been holding, and even though I can't put voice to it, I nod my head. *He likes my drawings.*

---

Aiden

WHEN SHE FINALLY NODS HER head, I flip to the beginning of the book and start at the first page. Her artwork is amazing. There are so many uplifting images of hope and dreams it floors me. But there's also sadness in some of them, images of caged birds with big sad eyes that I swear look just like Gracie's big, sky blue ones. Does she feel like a caged bird? The thought sickens me that she would feel anything but happiness. But when I finally get back to the image of the butterfly she wants tattooed on her body, I know I'm not wrong. The way she drew the butterfly in flight, with the same blue tones of her eyes, I know it's freedom she's yearning for, and as I hold her book to my chest, I vow to give it to her. I may not know her story, but I will before the night is over.

"Thank you for letting me look at these, Gracie. I would be honored to put this tattoo on you."

There's so much more I want to say. I want to demand answers, but I can tell she's worried about what I will think of her drawings, so I don't want to push her. She finally nods and I ask her, "Where do you want it?"

I hold my breath waiting for her to answer. It's already hard being this close to her; I don't know how I'm going to control myself when I get to touch her. She blushes from her chest all the way to her hairline. "I need to get it where people won't see it."

I suck in a breath, and then it hits me. "How old are you, Gracie?"

I say a silent prayer that she's of age. I don't know what I'll do if she tells me she's not.

"Eighteen." She says it so softly, I have to ask her again.

"How old?"

She blows a breath, tossing the hair on her forehead up. She reaches into her purse and pulls out a wallet, then holds it up to me. "See. I'm eighteen."

I take the wallet from her, not because I don't believe her but because I want to know more about her. Gracie Franklin, born July 5th, 2003. Her address is on Hightower Lane, and I knew before I even saw it that she was from the other part of town. "Today's your birthday."

She nods, and even though she smiles, it's a little sad. "I can pay you in cash... I can't use a card... I'm not supposed to be here."

I grip the wallet tighter in my hands. "Do you have a man?" I ask her gruffly, but even if she says yes, I'm not going to give her up. He's obviously not a good man if he let her come here on her own.

She shakes her head. "No, my father would have a fit if he knew I was here."

I sigh in relief. A dad I can handle. I couldn't handle a boyfriend. I hand her back her wallet and watch her put it back into her purse. "It's okay... I won't tell." *At least not yet.* But I don't say it out loud. She may have a controlling father, but she's eighteen, and I'm not going to let it go long without telling anyone that will listen that Gracie is mine. Even her father. "Plus, you're in luck. It's your birthday and I didn't get you anything. So the tattoo is on the house. My gift to you."

She looks at me skeptically. "That doesn't sound like a smart way to do business. You give tattoos away on birthdays? What's stopping people from just coming on their birthdays?"

I laugh because I can't help myself. I was right, she definitely is innocent. "Just you, baby. You're the only one getting free tattoos around here."

Her eyes widen. "But I can pay... just in cash."

I shake my head. "I'm not taking your money." *Fuck, baby girl, I should be paying you to touch your body.* I shake my head to try to keep the dirty thoughts at bay. There's no way I can tattoo her with a raging hard-on. "So where do you want it?"

She leans back in the chair on one arm. With her other hand, she points to her lower abdomen. "Here. But I need it so it will be covered by my panties or my bathing suit bottoms."

Fuck. Me. I'm not worried about a hard-on now. I'm pretty sure I'm about to come in my jeans.

## 3

## GRACIE

THIS IS CRAZY. I know it is. I'm being pulled in so many directions right now I don't know what the right thing to do is. My father could bust in here at any moment. I don't think he has a tracker on my phone, but who knows really? And if he does, I'm not the only one that will feel his wrath. Aiden will too, and I don't want that.

"Can you lock the door? I don't want... anyone to walk in while I have my dress up around my waist."

Aiden nods and walks over to shut and lock the door. The fluid movements from before are now jerky and stiff. "Are you sure about this? I really can come another day," I tell him, even though I know it's not true. I don't know when I'll get to come here again.

"We're doing this, Gracie. Unless you've changed your mind," he says gruffly as he starts doing something with the tools on the counter.

"I haven't changed my mind. I want you to put your mark on me."

He grunts and bends over his arms on the counter as he takes deep breaths. In and out, in and out. I'm about to ask him if he's okay when he turns toward me. His eyes are a dark blue now instead of the lighter teal from earlier. His jaw is tight as he moves next to me. "I want my mark on you."

I know we're talking about more than the tattoo, but all I can do is nod.

He blows out a breath. "Lift your dress, honey. Show me where you want it."

I lie back on the chair that is now more of a bed. I pull up my dress and cringe at the white cotton panties I have on. I definitely didn't think this through. "Right here," I say, pointing to my panties on my lower right hip.

He doesn't say a thing. He's staring at my lower body. His hand goes to my arm. "I'll have to pull your panties down a bit. Is that okay?"

I nod. "Yes, my bathing suit would have to cover it. If my dad... it just has to be covered," I explain. I let my head drop. I'm sure Aiden thinks I'm a child, all worried about what my father thinks or will do, but he doesn't know Mayor Franklin. Not like I do.

Aiden moves between my legs, lifting stirrups and removing the lower part of the table. This is how I would examine going to the gynecologist would be. He's standing between my spread legs, and there's strain on his face. "I'm going to free hand it if that's okay. Sometimes I use tracing techniques, but I'd like to replicate your drawing if that's okay."

I nod. "Sure, whatever you think is best."

I take a deep breath. I can't look away from him. His arms are covered in tattoos, and it makes me wonder where else he has them.

"You'll have to stop looking at me like that, Gracie. I'll never make it through this. Your eyes are telling me exactly what you're thinking."

I clench my eyes shut and lay my head back. I only open them when I know I'll be able to look at the ceiling instead of him.

My mind is whirling, waiting for his hands to be on me. When I feel them on each side of my hips, as if he's going to pull my underwear down, my hips flex in reaction and lift off the table as a moan escapes my lips. He freezes, and I do the same. Slowly, I let my hips fall back to the table.

## Aiden

Fuck. She's like a live wire. There's no way I'm going to last, not like this. She probably doesn't realize it, but her panties are soaked and almost transparent. They're stuck to her lips, and damn I'd give anything to put my mouth on her right now.

"Are you okay?" I ask her.

She lifts her arm and covers her face. She's embarrassed, and I don't want her to be. In a muffled voice, she says, "Yeah, I'm sorry. I don't know what's wrong with me. I've never... I don't know... It's weird.... I'm aching."

I'm going to hell... or I'm going to lose my license... One or the other or both, but I can't make myself care right now. "I can help you with that... help you relax."

She lifts her head. "I don't do drugs."

I laugh. I should probably be offended, but I'm not. "Me either, honey. No, I mean, you're wound tight... you need a release."

Her eyes squint in confusion, and if I didn't already know, I do now. She's a virgin. She's more innocent than any woman I've ever been around. All I can do is be thankful she came here today. "You're horny, Gracie," I tell her plainly.

Her eyes widen, and she starts to sit up and scoot backwards, instantly denying it. "I am not."

I nod my head, letting her move away from me when the whole time I want to hold her close. "Yes, you are. And it's fine. Let me make you feel good."

She's eyeing me skeptically. "Is this something you offer all your female clients? A tattoo with a side of... well, you know," she says awkwardly.

This time I do reach for her legs. I wrap my hands around her upper thighs. "No, I've never touched another client. It's sort of a rule I have."

"Why me?"

I tilt my head to the side. "Because I've never felt an attraction like this. You feel it too, right?"

She nods without even realizing it and then stops suddenly. "I'm not asking to fuck you, Gracie. Not yet." I slide my hand up her inner thigh. "I'll just use my hand. I want you to come. Then I'll be able to do your tattoo while you lie there limp and satisfied."

Her whole body is trembling. She needs this... she wants it but not more than I do. I want to see her come undone more than I've ever wanted anything in my life. I've almost reached the edge of her panties, and I stop there, stroking my finger back and forth along the edge. She shifts her body, pushing toward me, but I keep my finger right where it's at. "I'm not touching you until you tell me you want me to, baby."

"Yes," she mutters.

I smile, and instead of diving in like I want to, I ask her, "Yes what?"

She lifts her head up and meets my eyes. "Yes, I want you to touch me and make me feel good."

I nod. She's biting her lip again, something I'm realizing she does when she's nervous. When she lays her head back down, I put my thumb along the wet center of her panties. I stroke back and forth, gathering more moisture onto the already sodden material. Her whole body is pulled taut.

I slide her panties to the side, and she's all pink and glistening. I would give anything to put my mouth there and taste her. But I don't. I promised her with my hand only, and that's what I'll do. But I sure as hell will be licking my fingers after.

I separate her and stroke one thick finger through her wet, swollen folds. Her hips rise, and she whimpers. "You're already close, aren't you, Gracie?"

She shakes her head. "I don't know... I think."

I keep sliding my finger back and forth, and then paint her swollen clit with her desire. One touch on her nub, and she's already about to burst with pleasure. "Have you ever touched yourself, baby?"

She nods. "Yes, but not like this... I've never... I can't."

She's puffing out answers, but I'm able to make sense of it all. "You've never come before?"

She grunts, shaking her head again. She's so close. I slowly enter her, only knuckle deep, and pump a few times. I circle her clit, then rub back and forth over and over, increasing the pressure until her hips are so far off the table she has nowhere to go. She reaches down and grabs my wrist, but I don't release her or lighten my strokes. "Do you want me to stop?" I ask her. Sweat is pouring down my face. My cock is hard, and I'm pretty sure I'm about to come with her, but I don't care. Nothing matters now except for me giving Gracie her first orgasm.

"No. Don't stop."

I smile at her strangled command. "Come for me, Gracie. Let go, baby."

And that's it; she does exactly that. Her hips buck, but I keep stroking her. I want this to be everything for her and for her to never forget it. I want her to come to me when she needs her release. Only me.

She rides my hand, grunting and whimpering. I grunt with her, because my cock has a mind of its own and had to get in on the action too. I come in my jeans watching her orgasm. And when her hips fall to the table, I finally let her go.

She's limp on the chair. Her essence has filled the room, and I know I have to taste her. She lifts her hooded eyes, and when her gaze meets mine, I lift my fingers to my mouth, tasting her for the first time.

4

GRACIE

I'M STILL LYING HERE with my arm over my head, thinking. Aiden disappeared into the other room and came back shortly later with jogging pants on instead of the jeans from earlier. I couldn't help but notice when he first walked in, the way his pants were snug, outlining his manhood. He instantly caught me, and I should have known he would. "Eyes up here, Gracie. Or we'll never get this tattoo done."

I blushed to the roots of my hair and put my arm over my head again. And this is where I've stayed. Besides answering a few questions, I've lain just like this while Aiden tattooed me. It was uncomfortable at first, but nothing too bad. Plus, I can't think about that. All I can think about is what I let Aiden do. I believed him when he said he'd never done that to a client before. Maybe I'm just gullible, or maybe I wanted to believe him, I don't know. But I'll never regret what just happened. All my life I wanted to feel freedom, and I got my very first taste of it at the hands of Aiden Savage.

It seems like no time at all passes when he's telling me he's finished. He blots my skin, putting a thin layer of goo over it. He picks up a mirror off the counter and holds it, angling it so I can see the artwork. My hands go to my mouth. "It's perfect, Aiden. I love it."

He nods. "Well, it's perfect because your design is perfect. Can I take a picture?"

"To put in the book?" I ask him, worried that somehow my dad will find out.

"No, this is for my eyes only."

I nod, and he takes his phone and takes a picture. He goes over the care instructions and hands me a piece of paper that I fold up and clench onto.

Looking at my watch, I realize I have twenty minutes to get home before my father does. I jump off the bed, lowering my dress in the process. "I have to go.... my father."

Aiden wants to stop me; I can see he's surprised by my sudden need to leave, but he doesn't try to talk me out of it. "Let me walk you out to your car?"

"I walked. I have to hurry."

"Let me drive you," he says.

I'm shaking my head, stuffing the care instructions in my purse as I lift the strap over my shoulder. "No, I can't. I can walk."

"Gracie, stop," he demands, and I stop, looking up at him with a worried glance. "I'm not letting you walk all the way home. It's on the other side of town."

I roll my eyes. "Really, Aiden. This is Whiskey Run, not Jasper or anything."

But he's already wrapped his hand around mine, threading our fingers together. "I'm still not letting you walk. I'll take you home."

But I'm shaking my head. "If my dad..."

"Who is your father?"

I hang my head between my shoulders. "My father is Brandon Franklin."

"The mayor?"

I nod.

"Well, he seems like a decent enough guy. He wouldn't be happy that you're walking across town by yourself at dark. Let me just take you home."

"That's just it. He doesn't want me out, period. And with you? He would probably lock me in a room somewhere if I was seen unsupervised with a man. You can't drive me home."

He pulls me to him. "I'm not letting you walk. I'll drop you off close to home, but this isn't going to work, Gracie. I plan on seeing more of you, and I don't care who your father is, he's not going to stop me."

Hope flares in my chest. Man, I wish I could believe what he's saying. But no one bucks the wishes of Brandon Franklin. Nobody. I look at my watch again. "I have to go, Aiden."

<hr />

Aiden

"Do you trust me, Gracie?"

She doesn't even hesitate. "Yeah."

"Okay." I pull her with me as I lock up the shop and go out to my car. I don't release her until we're standing next to my F150. I open the door for her, gesturing for her to get in. She hesitates, and it goes all through me that she's this scared. Is it me, or is it the reaction from her father? "I'm not going to hurt you. I'll take you home. Drop you off down the road from your house."

She nods and climbs into my truck. I slam the door and walk around to get in. We're halfway across town before she says anything. "I'm not scared of you, Aiden."

My hand tightens on the steering wheel. "Who are you scared of?"

She shrugs. "It doesn't matter. Not really. I'm going to find a way to get away from my father."

"Does he hurt you?" I ask. I'm holding my breath, waiting for the answer. I may end up in jail tonight if I have to kill a man.

"No, not like that. He yells and stuff, but that's it. He's just controlling. I received a full scholarship to Berkeley, and he turned it down. He wants me to go to Jasper Community College and commute. I had hoped to get away from him, and now I don't know how."

I barely process what she's saying before I blurt it out. "You could stay with me. I could help you."

She shakes her head, and for the first time, I notice the sadness in her eyes. "I can't let you do that. He wouldn't let you... I know everyone thinks he's great and a good man, but he's not, Aiden. He's evil." I turn onto her street, and she points to a side street. "Pull in here. I'm just two houses down."

I do as she asks and turn off my truck. "You can't tell me he's an evil man and then just expect me to leave you like this."

"I'll be fine. He wouldn't hurt me." But even I can hear the doubt in her voice.

She reaches for the door. "Thank you for the ride... the tattoo... everything."

"Gracie, I wasn't lying earlier. I never do that with a client. I want to see you again."

She's shaking her head. "I'm not allowed to date."

I thread my fingers through her hair and grip the base of her neck, tugging her to me. I lean my forehead against hers. "That's not going to work for me, sweetie. I just tasted you on my fingers. You're mine now."

Her hands go to my chest, probably to push me away, but instead she bunches my shirt in her hand and pulls me even closer. I can't hold back anymore. I press my lips to hers in a first kiss that I feel all the way to my toes. "Open your mouth," I say against her lips, and she does what I ask.

I slide my tongue in and taste her. Her hands slide around my neck in a hard grip. Fuck, it's not enough. I pull her across the console, and she comes easily, her breasts flattened against my chest. I devour her, ravaging her, trying to get my fill, but at the same time, I know I never will. She's going to be mine.

It's damn near impossible to stop, but I know I have to. I pull away and look at her. Her lips are red and swollen; it's obvious what she's been doing. "We have to stop, or your dad will definitely know what you've been up to."

At the mention of her dad, she freezes and pulls away, moving back to her seat.

"I want to see you tomorrow."

"Aiden... I can't. I want to, but I can't."

"I'm not asking, Gracie. I will see you, if I have to come here to get you."

"No. Tomorrow is my dad's poker night. He's usually drunk and passed out by ten or eleven. I'll come to the shop after that."

I want to believe her. "Promise me. Promise I'll see you tomorrow."

She nods, her light blue eyes looking back at me. "I promise."

5

GRACIE

I walk into my house in a daze. My father's car is not in the driveway, so luckily I beat him home. I run up the stairs and into my bedroom. Dropping my purse on the bed, I go straight to my mirror over the dresser. The woman looking back at me looks almost unrecognizable to me. My hair is tussled, wild around my face. My eyes are shades darker, and my lips look puffy and bruised. I touch my fingers to my lips, remembering the kiss that Aiden gave me. With my hand over my heart, I try to catch my breath. I don't know how long I stand there just like that when my father opens my bedroom door.

He looks at me up and down, obviously noticing a difference in me. "Where have you been?"

I back away from the mirror. "I went for a walk."

"Don't lie to me, Gracie." His voice is stern and sounds lethal to me. He always does this, and it always intimidates me.

"I'm not lying. I did go for a walk."

He moves in close to me, and instead of pulling back like I normally would, I stay right where I'm at, jutting my chin at him.

He holds his phone up. "Explain this. Who is this?"

I gasp, looking at the picture. It's of me and Aiden sitting in his truck, when he kissed me. "How did you get that?" I ask, but I already know. From where it's taken, it was obviously our neighbor that took it and sent it to my father.

"I have spies everywhere. You can't do anything in this town without me knowing about it. Who is this man?" he asks, pointing at the phone.

"Just a friend, Dad. That's it."

His phone dings, and he raises it to his face. "Aiden Savage. Owner of Savage Ink. He is purchasing one of my buildings on the other side of town."

"Dad, he's just a friend."

He lifts his phone and points at it in disgust. "That is not just a friend. You are forbidden from seeing him, Gracie."

And for the first time in my life, I go against my father. "I'm eighteen now, Dad. I'm an adult. I can see whoever I want."

I suck in a breath as soon as I say it. The look he gives me is lethal, and even though he's never hit me before I fully expect him to do it by the way the vein is popping on the side of his neck.

His voice drops low. "No. You are still my daughter, and you will do as I say. If I ever catch you around that man again, I will destroy him. He'll lose his business and be run out of Whiskey Run so fast it will make your head spin. So if you like this man at all, you'll save him from this. Don't go near him again."

"But Dad..."

He puts his hand up. "No... as a matter of fact, you have three months until your college term starts at Jasper Community College. I'm sending you to your aunt's house."

I gasp. "In Kentucky?"

He nods. "Yes, Aunt Bethany will keep you on the straight and arrow until I let you come back. But you screw up, Gracie, and you'll never come back to Whiskey Run."

If he'd said those words to me yesterday, I would have been happy. But not now, not when I just met Aiden. "Dad, please don't do this."

He walks to my door and turns. "My mind is made up, Gracie. You disobey me in any way and I will destroy your friend. Everything he loves he will lose."

And then he slams the door behind him.

———

Aiden

THIS HAS BEEN the slowest day of my life. So many times I wanted to drive over to Gracie's house just so I could get a glimpse of her. But instead, I've kept myself busy. I spent the morning cleaning my apartment that is over top of the Savage Ink shop. Then from the afternoon into the evening I've been busy with one tattoo after another. When night finally comes, I'm on edge, pacing back and forth. Treyton and Dawson have already left for the day, leaving me to my anxious waiting.

I've thought about what I'm going to do if she doesn't show up. There won't be any stopping me. I know she's scared of how her father will react, but I won't let him stand in our way. I dreamed about

Gracie last night and the life we would have together. I know she's the one, and I'm not going to give up on us or our future.

When the clock strikes eleven and she's still not here, I grab my keys. I no sooner get out the front door of the shop and lock it up when I hear her. "Hey, Aiden."

"You came," I say stupidly. I had hoped she would and hadn't doubted it until the last hour or so.

"Yeah." She nods, looking over her shoulder as if she's being followed.

I stride toward her. "Are you okay?"

She nods, but instead of looking at me, she's looking down at the sidewalk. I walk toward her, holding out my hand. "Come on, my apartment is upstairs."

She reaches for me, and I wrap her hand in mine, taking her up the side stairs to my apartment. I open the door and hold my breath. I know this is nothing like her family home. The apartment has been decorated with furniture I got on sale at local stores. Nothing fancy and honestly, I've never worried about things like this before. But with Gracie, I do. I want her to like it here.

She walks into the room and straight to the wall of artwork. I've had a lot of my designs framed, and they're hanging on the wall in various forms. "Are these all yours?"

I nod and walk up behind her. She's staring up at them, pointing out what she likes about different ones, and I go to the side so I can see her face. But what I see shocks me. It was dark outside, and I totally missed this. "Gracie, what's wrong? Your eyes are swollen, your nose is red... what happened?"

She's shaking her head. "Nothing. Nothing is wrong."

But I don't believe her. I tilt her chin up with my finger. "Is it your dad? Did he upset you?"

She clenches her eyes shut tightly and nods. "Yeah, he did. But I'm here now, and I don't want to think about my dad."

I want to know so badly what is wrong with her, but she won't tell me. I don't want to upset her even more than she obviously already is. "Okay, but eventually you're going to have to tell me, Gracie. I'm not okay with sneaking around. I want everyone to know you're mine."

Her eyes widen. "But you just met me..."

I nod as I take a step toward her. I'm right up against her, and I can feel the brush of her breasts on my stomach with every breath she takes. "Yeah, I just met you... a little over twenty-four hours ago, but it's enough to know that I want you to be mine. There's a connection between us that I've never felt before, and I'm not going to let you go, Gracie. I want you."

Her hands go to my waist, and she tilts her head backwards. "Will you kiss me, Aiden?"

I lean down and press my lips to hers. I intend to go easy, but she's hungry for my touch, opening her mouth like I taught her to. Our tongues tangle against one another, and her hands are moving up and down my chest. She lifts my shirt, pressing her hands against my warm torso. I pull back, panting. "I didn't ask you here for this. We can wait. I don't want to rush you."

She's shaking her head before I can even finish. "I don't want to wait. Give me this, Aiden. Please, I need you."

I cup her jaw with my hand, stroking my thumb across her swollen lower lip. "Are you sure?"

She nods, and I lift her up into my arms. Her legs go around my waist, and I put my hands on her ass, holding her tightly against me. Already, my cock is hard, pressed against her hot, molten center. Our lips meet, and I forget everything else except the precious woman in my arms.

I carry her into the bedroom and sit down on the bed with her in my lap. She is pulling at my shirt almost desperately, and I lift my arms so she can take it off. She stares at me, her fingers tracing the ink on my body. Her touch is like a spark, causing a flame to shoot through my body. "I wondered..."

"Wondered what?" I ask, pulling her shirt over her head. Her breasts are large, pouring out of her white bra. Her nipples are hard, and I touch them through the thin material. She gasps, pressing her body into my hands.

She moans, and her head falls backwards. "I wondered if you were tattooed everywhere."

She leans back, looking at the trail of ink that disappears down the front of my pants. I shift, my cock harder from just having her look at me. "Yeah, almost everywhere."

She nods and reaches for the button of my jeans. "I want to see."

*Fuck, how am I going to survive this?*

6

GRACIE

HE STOPS me from undoing his pants and instead undoes my bra. He palms both my breasts, stroking his fingers over my hard peaks. I rock against him, feeling his hard cock underneath me. He may have gotten me distracted, but I won't be swayed this time. I don't have much time, and if I have to leave, I need this memory to get me through.

I reach between us, cupping his hardness in my hands. Even with the rough material of the jeans between us, I can still feel how big he is. He groans as he stands up and turns, laying me down on the bed. He makes quick work of removing my shoes and pants before discarding his own. By the time he lies down on me, my whole body is trembling at the contact.

Where he's hard, I'm soft. Where he has hair, I'm smooth, and every soft touch is like a tiny flicker that makes the blood rush to my head. I put my hands on his shoulders, and he's looking down, hovering over me. He's trying to read me, and although in most cases I'm an open book, I can't be tonight. I can't let him know that I'll be leaving Whiskey Run at daybreak and won't be back for three months. Hopefully, for fear of what will happen to him if he doesn't, I hope he does forget me. But there's a small part of me that knows he won't. I know what he means when he said this is special. It is special, and it's going to kill me leaving him. That's why I need this one night.

"I need you, Aiden.... please."

He slides his hand between us, moving his thick fingers through my wet and swollen folds. "You're soaking wet for me, Gracie."

I nod. "I know. I've thought about you... about this all day."

He leans down, his hot breath hitting my breast. "You're all I've thought about since yesterday." He suctions his lips to my nipples, and I arch my back on the bed.

He kisses down my belly, fitting his broad shoulders between my legs. He holds my legs open, and he's

41

almost salivating as he looks at my most private area. "I have to taste you, baby."

He doesn't wait for my response; he moves in, pressing his lips to my core. His tongue swipes through my folds as I clench the cover in my hands. He's doing more than tasting me. He's consuming me.

I lose all train of thought as I writhe underneath him. His strokes bring me to the edge and then he slows. Over and over, he torments me until I'm practically begging for him to let me come. I need that freedom that I felt yesterday. I yearn for it.

"Please," I beg him. "Please let me come."

He slides up my body and positions his manhood between us. I can feel him there, his hard thickness swaying back and forth over me. "I want you to come on my cock," he says as he kisses me. I can taste myself on him, but I'm not grossed out or disgusted; if anything, it brings me to a whole other level of desire.

"Yes. I want that too," I tell him, lifting my hips, trying to urge him on.

His head falls between my breasts, and he sighs before looking up at me. "I don't want anything between us, Gracie. I want to take you bare. I want to feel your silky, tight channel hugging me."

His gravely, demanding voice pulls at my lower belly. I feel like I could combust right now. "Yes, I want that too."

I know we should talk about things like protection, but right now, I don't even care. I want to feel him, all of him, inside me.

"I'm going to hurt you... but then I'm going to make you feel good."

His brow is creased, and I can tell it bothers him that he is going to have to cause me pain. But I don't care. Nothing can hurt as bad as knowing that I'll never have this again.

"I don't care. You can do whatever you want to me, Aiden. I want it all. Please."

He looks at me, no doubt wondering about the desperation in my voice, but I don't give him time to think about it. I open my legs wider and shift my body so he's lined up at my entrance. "Please..."

He pushes into me, barely an inch. "You're so fuckin' tight, baby."

I groan at the intrusion on my body. I feel full already, but I know there's more, and I want to experience it all. "Please, Aiden. Hurt me, please, get it over with and then make me feel good. I need to feel good," I plead with him.

He plunges into me in one quick thrust. I gasp, and I can't stop the tears from forming in my eyes if I tried. He's buried inside me, fitted right up against me, and I struggle to catch my breath. My eyes clear, and I hear him telling me he's sorry over and over. He's kissing my eyes, whispering against my lips. "Gracie, baby, tell me you're okay."

I nod. "I'm fine, but make me feel better, Aiden."

He reaches between us and goes straight to my clit. I'm already on fire and fully aroused, but his motions take me to the next level. I start to lift my hips, adjusting to the feel of him inside me. "Yes," I breathe against his lips.

He smiles. "That's my girl." And just those few words go straight to my heart. I want that more than anything. I wish I could be his girl.

He starts to move then, and what I thought was good before was nothing compared to this erotic friction that feels like it might combust between us. His hips move up and down, and he never stops the torture on my clit. "I'm close," I sigh.

"Come for me, Gracie. Come for me."

I do, and the orgasm rushes through my body like a rocket. I can feel him everywhere, touching and pleasing me, taking me higher than I've ever been before. He's grunting, his face clenched when he comes too, grunting into my neck as his body convulses.

We're both panting. I have my arms wrapped around him, and I'm probably being too clingy, but I don't care. We won't have tomorrow, so right now I'm going to try to memorize the feeling of being in his arms.

"Are you okay?" he asks, pulling back enough to look into my eyes.

I nod. "I'm good. I'm really good, actually."

He raises himself up, and I grimace as he pulls from me.

"Stay right there, I'll be right back."

He walks away, and I watch his naked body as he moves. He wasn't kidding. He really is tattooed everywhere.

He comes back shortly, and I can't help but stare at his muscular body with his manhood still semi hard between his legs. He stops next to the bed, and I raise my eyes to his when I realize he's watching me.

"I would give anything to have you again, but I know I would really hurt you then. You need to recover."

## Aiden

MY DICK TWITCHES as she stares at it. I would love to be inside her again, but I know it would hurt her if I took her again so soon.

I go around the bed, between her legs. She reaches for the warm rag in my hands, but I don't let it go. I want to be the one to take care of her. "I want to do it. Open your legs, Gracie."

She does, but almost shyly as if I wasn't balls deep inside her just minutes ago. Her pussy is red, and the remnants of her virginity and our cum is leaking out of her. I don't know why, but the image bothers me. I take my finger and push the jizz inside her. I then take the warm cloth and clean her gingerly. As soon as I'm done, I toss the cloth into the hamper and then climb into the bed beside her, pulling her naked body against mine. I know I should cover her up because she is way too tempting, but I need to have her in my arms.

She comes to me easily, and I wrap our arms and legs around each other. Her eyes are hooded, and I know she's tired.

"Are you okay?"

She nods and yawns softly. "I'm really good. Thank you for tonight, Aiden. I'll never forget this."

"I'm glad you enjoyed it because now that I've had you, I won't be able to keep my hands off you, Gracie."

She looks surprised.

"I dreamt of us last night. It was about our future. I know it's too soon, but I'm going to tell you about it one day because it felt so real. For the first time ever, I want to settle down and buy a house, start a family."

Her eyes widen, and I'm sure I'm freaking her out. She just lost her virginity and already I'm talking about getting her pregnant. "Don't worry, we have all the time in the world. Let's just enjoy tonight."

She snuggles closer, and I want her to talk to me; I love hearing her voice. "Tell me more about you. What do you want to do with your life?"

She shrugs, and I lean back to look in her eyes. "Really, if you could do or be anything, what would that be?"

She doesn't hesitate this time. "I'd be an artist. I would love to be able to make art and have it hanging in galleries or even in people's homes. I just want to be able to share my work."

Her eyes light up as she's talking about her art, and I know exactly how she feels. I'm the same way about my tattoos. I love giving people a way to express themselves. "You should do it, Gracie. Just the artwork I've seen is amazing. You really do have a gift."

Her chest expands against me as she takes a deep breath. "Yeah, maybe someday."

"I can help you get started. I have savings."

"I'm not taking your money, Aiden."

I shake my head. I know it's soon. She doesn't get it or understand that I want her to be mine, and that means anything that is mine is hers. I don't want to ruin it tonight. We have forever to work it out. "Well, the offer stands. I know you can make a success with your art. I'm just offering to help, that's all."

She kisses my chest and lays her head down on my shoulder. I can't explain the look on her face, but there's still a tinge of sadness in her eyes. I wish I could wipe it away, but the only way that is going to be possible is to get her away from her father.

She smiles, but it doesn't quite reach her eyes. "You don't know how much it means to me that you believe in me."

I pull her tighter against me. "Always. I'll always believe in you."

She looks like she might say something, but when she closes her eyes and buries her head into my chest, I leave it be. I lay my chin on her head and fall asleep with my future in my arms.

7

GRACIE

I snuck out on him. I had to. I know I wouldn't be
able to leave and lie to him if he was awake and
looking at me. I waited until he'd finally fallen
asleep, and I carefully pulled from his arms. I don't
know how long I sat there, staring at him, memo-
rizing everything about him before I made myself
get up. I dressed as quietly as I could before I pulled
the already written letter from my purse and set it
on his nightstand. He is going to hate me after
reading it. I know he will, but it's for his own good.
There's no way I could just let my dad destroy him
and his business, and that's exactly what he'd do if I
tried to see Aiden again.

I was selfish and wanted one night with him, so
that's what I did. Maybe when I come back in three
months, things can be different. Maybe I can appeal

to my dad and he will have a change of heart. But even as I'm thinking it, I know it won't happen. There is no future for Aiden and me, and the sooner I come to terms with it the better off I will be.

I walk all the way back to my house and sneak into my bedroom. I'm a nervous wreck, knowing I could be caught, but this was a chance I had to take. I couldn't just leave Whiskey Run without seeing Aiden again.

I fall into my bed and look at the clock. I have to be up in two hours. My father is putting me on a plane to Kentucky. I've already made plans. I'm going to find a way in the next three months to get free from my father. I won't be able to come back to Whiskey Run, but maybe, if Aiden doesn't completely hate me, I could get him to come visit me. That's the only hope I'm able to hold on to. I have to do something because I can't live like this.

<hr />

## Aiden

THE SUN IS BARELY RISEN, and I sit up, knowing something isn't right. I'm still naked from the night before, but instead of feeling the heat of Gracie's body next to mine, I feel chilled. The apartment is quiet, and I know that no one is here. She left.

I raise up and notice the letter on the nightstand immediately. It's folded, and in big cursive writing it has my name on the front of it.

I reach for it, unfold it and start to read, with a feeling of dread already in the pit of my stomach.

*Dear Aiden, I'm sorry to do this in a letter but I can't see you anymore. Actually, I don't want to. Thank you for last night, but I knew all along that it could only be one night. We're not really a good fit; you and I just don't make sense. I'm going out of town for the summer so hopefully when I come back, you will have forgotten about me. Please don't come for me. I don't want to see you again. Gracie*

I read it again, over and over. None of it makes sense. She's completely blowing me off, but what she doesn't realize is I was there last night... right there with her. I could feel what I mean to her when she kissed me and when she gave me her virginity.

I read the letter again, wondering if I'm missing something. I look at the cursive letters of her name. She dotted her "I" with a heart and that one lone heart gives me hope. I'm going to give her a few days to cool off, and then I'm coming for her. She thinks we're not a good fit. Fuck that, she's the only one for me.

8

GRACIE

NINE MONTHS LATER

"AUNT BETHANY, I can't go back to Whiskey Run. You know my father. He'll make good on his promise to hurt Aiden."

"Sit down," she says in a stern voice. I dreaded coming to Bethany's house in Kentucky. I had assumed that I would be kept a prisoner here, just like I was in Whiskey Run, but that hasn't been the case at all. The first few months I was here, Bethany was pretty strict, especially when my father would come and visit. But after that, she let me do the things I wanted to do. And well, when I found out I was pregnant she's done everything possible to help me and protect me from the wrath of my father. She enrolled me in the local college here and she even let me take a few art classes from a gallery downtown. I think my father was relieved that I was

53

out of his hair. He's been on edge lately when I've talked to him.

I do as she asks and sit down on the couch. She sits across from me and holds my hand. "You still love this Aiden, don't you?"

I nod instantly. I knew him for a little over twenty-four hours, but I know I'll never love anyone the way I love him. I put my hand on my belly, wishing I could tell him about the life we made together that one night together but knowing I can't.

"Okay, you need to go back to Whiskey Run, and you need to talk to him."

I pull my hand back from Bethany. "I can't. My father..."

Bethany is shaking her head. "Listen to me. Your father knows you're pregnant. We hid it for as long as we could, but someone from here talked to him and asked him if he was excited to be a grandfather."

Panic rises in my chest. I know it was foolish to think I could hide this from him. But I'd at least hoped to keep it a secret until after the baby was born. "Oh my God. Oh my God."

Bethany jerks on my hand and cups my jaw, forcing me to look at her. She's holding on to me tightly, telling me that she's scared of my father as well. "Listen to me. Your father is on his way here. He plans to take you from here and is going to put the baby up for adoption. You have to leave."

I put my arms over my rounded stomach and gasp. "No!"

"Gracie, we don't have much time. If he's flying, he'll be here soon. Throw some water on your face. Pack some food to take, and I'm going to pack your clothes. Try and be calm. The stress is not good for the baby."

I start to get up, but with all the added weight it's difficult, so Bethany helps me. "But what about you? I can't leave you here to deal with him."

"I'll be fine. You only need to worry about you and that baby. Now get to packing and be ready to go in ten minutes."

I nod and walk off toward the kitchen as she goes up the stairs to my room. A part of me is going to be sad to be leaving here. Bethany has turned out to be the best friend I ever had. She's protected me and loved me so much these past nine months. She's butted heads with my father over and over but has stood her ground to keep me safe from him.

I pack the food and drinks and use the bathroom. I am no sooner done than Bethany comes down with

HOPE FORD

two suitcases packed full. I follow her outside and see that she is putting everything in her car. "Bethany, I can't take your car. Put it in mine."

She doesn't stop though. "No. I have new tires, and mine is a lot safer. I don't want to worry about you on the road. Just take it."

"But..."

She's shaking her head. "Think about the baby, Gracie. Everything else we'll figure out later. For now, just do what's right for the baby."

When I finally agree, she finishes loading the bags, and as soon as she closes the trunk, I grab on to her. The tears have already started. "I'm going to miss you so much, Aunt Bethany."

She hugs me back tightly. "I'm going to miss you too, child." She pulls back and searches my face. "Gracie, there's things you don't know about your father... bad things. Don't let him get a hold of your baby. Whatever he tells you, don't trust him. Protect your daughter from him."

My eyes round. I knew my father was an evil man, but I never dreamed he would do anything to hurt a grandchild of his very own. Am I naïve to think he wouldn't hurt my baby?

Bethany shakes my shoulders, obviously seeing the doubt on my face. "I didn't want to tell you like this, but your father is involved in human trafficking. I've already reported everything I know to the FBI, but until it's investigated, you and your baby are not safe, Gracie. Please believe me."

She has no reason to lie, and even I can hear the desperation in her voice. "I promise, Bethany. I'll protect her. My father won't get anywhere near her... ever."

She nods, satisfied. "Now go and be safe. Call me when you get there."

"Come with me, Bethany. I don't want you to deal with—"

"No, I'm staying and I'm going to buy you some time. Go to Aiden. He'll protect you both."

I take a deep breath. "He probably hates me."

Aunt Bethany is shaking her head, opening the door and practically pushing me into the driver's seat. "He loves you, and eventually he'll understand why you did what you did."

I nod, wiping the tears. "I love you."

She pats my arm through the window. "I love you too, Gracie. There are things for the baby in the back seat. Enough to get you started, but I'll come see you soon."

"Thank you for everything."

She backs away from the car and starts to wave. I wave back and back out of the driveway. The drive from here to Whiskey Run should take me a little less than four hours, but the time goes fast because all I can think about is Aiden. I'm worried that I'm bringing grief to his door, but I also know that I don't have a choice. I have to protect our daughter.

---

## Aiden

IT'S ANOTHER FRIDAY NIGHT, and I'm at work. It seems that's all I do anymore. Well, that, search for Gracie, and keep Mayor Franklin under surveillance. That's all I've done for the past nine months. My head falls between my shoulders, and I try to suck in a deep breath...fuck. I still feel like I'm drowning. I lift the tattoo gun and switch it off.

"You okay, brother?" Treyton asks. He's my best friend, and he also works at Savage Ink. I'm working on his back tattoo, something that I've been trying to get finished between clients for the past month. I promised him that I would get it done tonight, and I will if I can keep my mind off Gracie.

"Yeah, I'm good. Just need to stretch. Want a water?" I ask him as I stretch my arms over my head as if I really had a cramp. The truth is, when I start thinking about Gracie, my hands start to twitch. And a tattoo artist with an unsteady hand is not a good thing.

The look Treyton gives me tells me that he can see right through me. He knows how messed up I've been. I don't even know why I'm acting. "I'm good, man. Take your time."

I walk out of the room and into the breakroom, taking deep breaths. I've been like this since the day Gracie left Whiskey Run, and I don't see it getting better anytime soon. It's like I have something heavy lying on my chest, and no matter what I do to try and relieve it, it's still there, reminding me that she's gone... that she left me.

As if I need any fuckin' reminders. My whole world turned black when she made the decision she didn't want me. Treyton and Dawson think I'm crazy to react like I have over a girl I knew for a little over twenty-four hours, but I can't explain it. I fell in love...and I fell hard. I gave her a few days to cool down, and I went to her house to find out from her father that she'd left Whiskey Run. She had her fuckin' dad tell me she was gone and I was just supposed to be okay with it. Well, I wasn't. I'm still not. I've searched everywhere for her. She left without a trace, and as far as I can tell, she hasn't stepped foot back in Whiskey Run since the day she left. As a matter of fact, I know she hasn't. I've pretty much stalked her father's house and made a damn nuisance of myself. But I don't care. None of that matters. Nothing matters if I don't have Gracie.

"Aiden!" Treyton hollers from the other room. "I have a client coming in soon. Let's get this done."

I lift my hand in front of me, but unfortunately the tremors are still there. I shake it but know it's not going to help. I make a fist and holler, "Be right there."

I chug the rest of the water wishing it was something stronger. A good shot of whiskey right now would do the trick. Too bad I never drink and tattoo. On the way out of the breakroom, I throw the bottle in the recycle bin and look at my reflection in the mirror on the wall. I look like a tortured man; I've aged twenty years in nine months. "Fuck!" I say under my breath. "Get it together, Aiden."

I walk back toward my area, still stretching my arms. "Sorry about that. Let's get it going."

Treyton grunts; no doubt he's fed up with my shit. So am I. Trust me, if I could forget about Gracie I would. But it's not possible.

I pick up the tattoo gun and get back to work, leaning my wrist on Treyton's shoulder blade to help steady my hand. It's not a technique I like to use, but it works.

I barely get started when my phone starts to ring. I should ignore it—I've already stalled enough—but since Gracie's left, I haven't let one phone call go to voicemail. I don't want to miss her call in case she does ever decide she wants to talk to me again.

I don't turn off the gun because I'm determined to just find out who it is and tell them I'll call them back. One look at the caller ID and I see Tate Jennings' name. He's a friend. I've given him a tattoo once or twice and he's saved my ass one time after Gracie left and I was on a drunken binge and about to destroy everything at the Whiskey Whistler Bar.

"Hello."

"Hey, Aiden, this is Tate."

I move the phone to hold against my shoulder. "What's up, man? I'm kinda in the middle of something. Can I call you back?"

His sigh is loud on the phone, and the tone in his voice tells me that something isn't right. "No, it can't wait. I, well, thought you should know that Gracie's here..."

I turn the gun off and jump up. Treyton turns to me with a question but doesn't say anything. His stare levels me, and I have no doubt he's on high alert ready to go if something is going down. "In Whiskey Run?" I ask, not even recognizing my own voice.

He pauses, and it takes all I have to remain silent while I wait for him to respond. "Uh, actually no. At the hospital in Jasper."

My stomach plummets, and I can feel myself getting sick. "Fuck! It will take me thirty minutes to get there. Is she okay?"

Tate stammers, "Uh, yeah, as far as I know she's okay."

I tighten my hold on the phone and grab my keys off the counter. "Don't let her leave. I'm coming."

I hang up the phone before I even think to ask what floor she's on or where she's at. "I'm sorry, Trey. I have to go."

"Gracie?" he asks while he follows me out to my truck.

"Yeah, she's in the hospital... fuck... I don't even know what's happening, I'll have to call Tate back. I have to go."

"Let me drive you."

"I'm fine. Can you cancel my appointments for me?"

He nods, and I drive off toward Jasper.

The thirty-minute drive gives me plenty of time to think, and every thought is about Gracie. We were good together, damn we were so good together. The attraction was instant for both of us, and from that moment I knew she was going to be my wife. I know it's crazy, but even now, even after she walked away from me, left me with only a note, I would marry her tomorrow if she'd have me. It makes me sound like a punk ass that is pussy whipped, but I don't care. There's nothing or nobody that matters to me like Gracie does. First, I'm going to make sure she's all right. Then I'm going to find a way to keep her with me for always.

9

GRACIE

"Yeah, we're in room 312, but I should probably..."

Tate pulls the phone from his ear and then pockets it. I jut my chin at him because I know who was on the other end of that phone call. "That was Aiden, right? You called him and told him I was here."

I know it sounds like I'm accusing him, but I'm not. The whole situation is messed up, and this is not how I intended for Aiden to find out he is going to be a father.

I was on my way to Savage Ink. I was going to tell Aiden about the baby, and even though I've had almost four hours to figure out how I was going to do it, I still didn't have a clue. Maybe this is best.

He's going to know as soon as he lays eyes on me anyway.

When I started having pains, I thought it was just Braxton-Hicks again, but the worse they got, I knew I needed to get checked out. I never dreamed they would admit me and that I was already three centimeters dilated.

Tate crosses his arms on his chest. He is the mechanic in Whiskey Run, and his sister is Violet, who owns Red's Diner. They are good people, so I can't really be mad at him. "Yes, I called and told him. Violet saw you when you came in, and that's why she sent Lakelyn and me over here to see you and to call Aiden. She didn't want you to be alone."

I can't help but smirk. That's definitely Violet. She worries about everyone, and it's just like her to want to make sure Aiden was here. She's probably trying to do her matchmaking thing like she's done with half the town, but it's not going to work on me and Aiden. I really screwed it up with him, and he probably doesn't even want to see me. But right now, I'm going to accept my fate.

"How is Violet? She doing okay?"

Tate nods. "She's fine, and Josh Jr. is doing great too."

If anyone deserves happiness, it's Violet. "That's great. I only got to see her for a minute, but she looked good... happy."

Tate nods, and I can feel the pity from across the room.

I lift my chin. "When will Aiden be here?"

Tate sighs. "He's parking his truck right now."

I nod and look over at the woman that came in with Tate. She's beautiful, and for some reason she looks familiar. "Lakelyn, I'm sorry we met like this, but for some reason, I feel like I've seen you before."

She smiles softly at me and shrugs.

Tate reaches for her and grabs her hand. "She's a model and has done some commercials. That could've been it."

"Oh yeah, the..." But before I can mention seeing her in the clothing commercial I stop as another contraction hits me.

I've done really well at working through them, but this one is nothing like the others. My whole body flexes. Tate steps away from the bed as Lakelyn, bless her, walks closer to me, offering her hand. I grab on to it and listen to her soothing voice. "Breathe, Gracie. You got this."

My whole body is drawn tight when there's a loud knock on the door and it seems simultaneously the door swings open. There's no way that Aiden was prepared for what he's seeing. All the color leaves his body; even his tattoos look like an ashy gray instead of a vibrant black, and I swear he sways on his feet. This is definitely not the way I pictured it. I had hoped to look pretty. Instead, I'm in bed, big and swollen, drenched in sweat, and no matter how much I want to, I can't erase the pain on my face.

He walks toward me, and even though I have so much I need to say to him, there's no way I can start now. "Breathe, Gracie. It's okay. Keep breathing."

My eyes are on Aiden because I can't look away. He's upset. Most people probably wouldn't notice, but I do. His jaw is set, and even though he's regaining some of his color, he's staring at me as if I have two heads instead of like I'm about to give birth to his child.

The pain starts to lessen, and I slowly start to sit back. I'm still gripping Lakelyn's hand, and her fingertips are white from how hard I held on to her. I release her quickly. "I'm so sorry, Lakelyn."

She shakes her head like it's not a big deal, but I notice she's rubbing her hands together as if she's trying to get the feeling back. "No, it's fine. That was a rough one. Are you okay? Can I get you anything?"

She's looking at me, concern etched on her face. She's completely ignoring the man that just walked in, and I sort of wish I could do the same. I'm still panting, but I'm able to get it out. "Ice chips... please."

She nods and walks out of the room. Tate is standing in the corner, his eyes on Aiden, and I reluctantly look up at him.

Tate clears his throat. "I'm going to go help Lake. We'll be back."

But neither Aiden nor I acknowledge him. I'm too busy taking in all of Aiden. Fuck, how I missed him. I've thought of this moment a thousand times. He came to me in my dreams every night for nine months, but this is reality, and I can't expect him to just forgive me in an instant.

"Were you going to tell me?" he asks.

His voice is thick, deeper than normal, telling me how much emotion is going through him right now. At least he didn't ask me if the baby was his. That would have killed me. But surely he knows; I gave my virginity to him. There's no way I would have ever slept with someone else.

I take a deep breath. "I was on my way to Whiskey Run to tell you, but I had to make a stop at the hospital first... I didn't want you to find out like this."

He grips the railing on the bed. "If I had to guess, you didn't want me to know at all. What? Did the guilt get to you... leaving me like you did?"

It guts me to know how much I hurt him. "There are things you don't know. I was coming to tell you... I need you."

He leans toward me. His voice is deep and steady. "I needed you these last nine months, Gracie. I've been lost without you... You wrote me a damn note to tell me I wasn't good enough for you."

I can feel the pull in my lower belly as another contraction starts. It's too soon. Didn't the other one just finish? I grip my belly and try to tell him. "I had to, Aiden. I didn't have a choice."

His face tightens, and he's so mad he spits the words out. "There's always a choice, Gracie."

"Ohhhhhh!" I scream, holding my belly. "Oh God!" I say as the contraction hits harder. Aiden grabs my hand, and I squeeze fighting through the pain.

"Breathe, Gracie. Keep breathing."

He no sooner gets the words out than the door swings open. The doctor that checked me earlier walks in the room with Tate and Lakelyn following behind. "Well, it seems they are getting closer and more intense."

I nod, grunting through the pain.

Lakelyn presses a cold wet towel to my head, which is surprisingly soothing.

I keep grunting, doing my best to work and breathe through the pain. All eyes are on me, and I try to take deep breaths until finally it subsides, and I fall back onto the bed.

The doctor is watching a monitor. "That one was a doozy. Let me check your dilation."

Instantly, Tate and Lakelyn step back outside the room as the doctor sits down on a stool between my legs. Aiden is still holding my hand, and even though I know he probably hates me right now, I can't let him leave me. Our daughter and I need him more than ever.

The doctor's head raises, and instantly I see the crease of his forehead. "You're still at three centimeters. We're going to have to do a C-section, Gracie. I know you didn't want an epidural, and it's too late for that, but we will have to use an anesthetic for the surgery. Someone will be in shortly to get you prepped."

"But I wanted to do this naturally."

The doctor comes up and stands next to my head. "I know you did, but that monitor there is letting us know how the baby is doing. She's starting to get a little distressed, and she is ready to come out. The safest way for you and baby is to do it this way."

Everything is so confusing. I'm exhausted and trying to piece it all together. "And I have to be out?"

He smiles. "Yes, and trust me, you'll want to be for this."

I nod, and the doctor grips my shoulder. "I've done thousands of these. You and your baby girl are going to be fine." He raises his head. "Are you the father?"

I cringe, waiting for Aiden's response.

"Yes, I'm the father."

"Okay, I'm assuming you want to be in there."

Aiden gulps. "Yes."

"Great, the nurses will instruct you on what you need to do."

He nods, and I watch as the doctor leaves.

It hits me then that there's not much time, and there's so much to say. "Aiden, I know that you probably hate me. I know we have a lot to talk about, but I need you to make me a promise."

He is still holding my hand, and there's no trust in his eyes as he stares back at me. "What is it?"

"Well, I didn't want to be out. I needed to have a clear head and be able to take care of our daughter, but if they're putting me out, I can't. I need you to take care of her."

"Gracie, I don't know how to take care of a baby, but I promise I will make sure she's fed and taken care of. You'll be back with her soon enough. You can teach me and show me what I need to do."

"No, you don't understand," I say in frustration. "I'm telling you, do not let her out of your sight. If my father shows up, don't let him near her."

The nurse comes in and starts moving the IV poles, disconnecting and reconnecting tubes. "My father will sell her, Aiden. Promise me that you will protect her while I can't. Promise me," I ask in urgency as the nurse asks if I'm ready.

Aiden was mad when he walked in, but now he looks downright lethal. He leans down and puts his hand softly to my face. "From this point on, I will protect you and our daughter, Gracie. Nothing is going to happen to either of you. He won't come near either of you ever again."

The way he's looking at me, like I'm his whole life, makes me believe what he's saying.

The monitor starts to buzz, and the nurse cuts in. "We have to move." She tosses a scrub to Aiden. "Put this on and follow us."

10

AIDEN

GRACIE IS BACK... and I'm a father.

I stayed right with her through the whole delivery.
They tried to get me out once the baby was born,
and I had to make the hardest decision of my life. I
had to leave Gracie to be with our daughter while
they weighed her and took care of her. The nurse
assured me Gracie would be fine, and so I did what
I promised Gracie I would do. I stayed with our
daughter.

Gracie has been in recovery for a little over an hour,
and my daughter and I are already back in the
room. The nurse has been teaching me things, how
to change her, how to wrap her in a blanket, and
basically how to care for her. I have my shirt off
with the baby held to my chest. The nurse said that
this brings babies comfort until their mothers are

able to hold them, so I didn't hesitate. I just met her, but I'd do anything for our baby.

The nurse pulls out a small bottle and tries to hand it to me, but with my arms full of my daughter, I shake my head. I didn't have time to talk to Gracie about this, but I'm almost positive she would want to breast feed her.

"Should I give her that? I think Gracie would want to breastfeed her."

The nurse shrugs like it's not a big deal. "It will be fine, she still can if she wants to."

Fuck, I don't know anything about this, but for some reason it doesn't feel right. "Since she's sleeping," I say, nodding my head at the baby in my arms, "can we wait until she wakes up? Maybe Gracie will be here by then and she can decide."

The nurse harumphs at me, obviously not liking the fact that I'm bucking her but finally agrees. "Fine, I'll be right out in the hall if you need anything."

I nod, but all my attention is focused on my daughter. She's sleeping so peacefully, nothing like a squalling baby that I somehow had pictured a newborn to be. I stroke my finger softly across her cheek and she twitches, and I swear it looks like she's smiling in her sleep.

"Oh baby girl, how could I just find out about you and already love you this much? Your mommy took good care of you; they said you are a perfectly healthy baby. Now it's my turn, now I'm going to take care of you and your momma."

I sniff and wipe at the tear in my eye. I don't know what's going on, but I know without a shadow of a doubt that Gracie leaving me had something to do with her father. I'm still mad... I can't believe she just left the way she did, but I can't deal with that now. There are more important things at hand.

The door opens, and a nurse wheels in a groggy Gracie. As soon as the wheels on her bed get locked in, I stand up and walk over to the side of it.

The nurse grabs the clipboard off the end of the bed and holds it to her chest. "She's groggy, but you can wake her up. Don't let her up without one of us or you to help her."

I nod, never taking my eyes off Gracie. She's exhausted, and I can't even begin to imagine how she did all this on her own. "Gracie, baby. There's someone here wanting to meet you."

"Aiden?" she asks, forcing her eyelids open.

"Yeah, I'm right here, and I have our baby. Do you want to hold her?"

Her eyes pop open, and her bright blue eyes are staring at me. She looks at the baby against my chest and starts to cry. "Oh my, she's perfect. She's just perfect, Aiden."

I nod and sniff, feeling every emotion she is. "She is perfect. Do you want to hold her?"

She wipes at her eyes. "I do, I really do. But look at me." She holds her hand out, and it's shaking so bad.

"What's wrong? Do you want me to get the nurse?"

She shakes her head. "No, it's the aftereffects of the anesthesia. But I don't want to drop her."

She wants to hold her so bad I can see it. "I'm going to help you. I'll stay right here, and I won't let anything happen to her, Gracie. I promise."

Our eyes meet, and finally she nods, holding her hands out to me. I nod at the gown she has on. "Do you want to pull your gown down a little? The nurse said the heat and our heartbeat helps soothe them."

She pulls the sleeves down, and I do my best to ignore the large rounded breast she flashes me as she pulls it down and then uses the gown to cover her breast again. When she's situated, I lay our baby on her chest and she seems to take a deep breath, sigh, and then go right on sleeping.

I give Gracie time with her. I stand next to the bed, but I let Gracie count her fingers and toes, touch her hair and cheek. Everything I did when I first met our little miracle.

Gracie looks up at me. "Did I traumatize Lakelyn and Tate?"

I laugh. "Tate definitely looked uneasy about it all, but I'm pretty sure Lakelyn was fine. I thanked them for taking care of you until I got here. They said they'll stop in and see you when they come see Violet."

The silence builds as we look at one another. She blinks up at me, tearfully. "I'm sorry for what I did and how I left. I didn't want to, but I really didn't have a choice."

I take a deep breath. I didn't want to do this now. I wanted her to recover before we get into all of it, but obviously she wants to get it off her chest. "You always have a choice, Gracie." She rears back suddenly, and the baby starts to cry.

Gracie's eyes go big, and I know the medicine in her body is still making her groggy and not altogether with it. "She's probably hungry."

The screams get louder just as the nurse comes in. "Well, it looks like our little lady is hungry. Do you want the bottle now?"

Gracie instantly shakes her head. "No, I'd like to try and feed her myself." Her cheeks turn pink.

Gracie lowers the gown and moves our baby to her breast. She instantly starts to root and suck at her. I'm in awe, and I can't take my eyes off them. I don't know how long I stand there before Gracie nudges me. "Will you put a shirt on?"

I had forgotten that I was still without my shirt. I look at her questioningly, and she grimaces and nods at the nurse. I look at the nurse and instead of watching mom and baby, she's watching me. I walk back over to the chair and pull my shirt on. "I think we're good, right, Gracie? You need anything, baby?"

I can tell she appreciates the endearment. "No, I think I have everything I need."

I nod, and the nurse leaves in a huff.

I lean down on the bed to watch them. "Have you picked out a name?"

She shakes her head and shrugs. "I had a few but wasn't dead set on any of them. Now that you're here, I think we should pick it together."

I brush the hair off her face and smile at her. "I think that's a great idea." I reach for the paperwork they left with me earlier and hold it up for her to see. "I filled out all the information I know."

"You remembered my birth date?"

"Yeah, I met you on your eighteenth birthday."

She scans the paperwork. "You put your address in Whiskey Run as my address."

"I sure did. Because that's where you and baby Savage are going after here. I know it's not much."

"Aiden, don't say that. I want to stay with you, but there are things you don't know. Things that may change your mind about me and our baby."

I pull the chair up to the bed. "Okay, name. We can't keep calling her baby. Let's do that first."

She nods. "What are you thinking?

"How about Jessica?" I ask.

She gasps. "That's my mother's name."

I stroke my hand up and down her arm. "I know. When you left, I did everything to find out every-thing I could about you and your family. I know you were close to her. But if it's going to be a bad reminder—"

"No! I love it, thank you Aiden."

I use my other hand to stroke along Jessica's back. "So Jessica it is."

Gracie nods and lifts Jessica higher to softly tap on her back to burp her. I try not to stare at Gracie's uncovered breast. "Okay, so that's settled. So I know that you have some kind of secret or something that you think is going to change how I feel about you."

She nods, but before she can say anything, I hold my hand up. "I'm going to let you tell me what this is so we can take care of it. But I want you to know right now, there's nothing that you can say that will change how I feel about you. You are mine, Gracie. You were mine nine months. I'm going to take you and Jessica home with me, and I'm going to give you the best life. We are going to buy a house, get married and probably have more babies if you're up to it."

11

GRACIE

OH MY GOD, he's saying all the right things. But how can I do this to him? Possibly destroy his whole life just so I can be with him.

I shake my head about to tell him to forget it when Jessica sighs against my neck.

But he's already shaking his head. "That's how, Gracie. It's not just about you anymore. You have to think about your daughter." So in one rush I lay it all out for him.

"My father found out about you and me. He sent me away and told me if I came near you that he would destroy your business and run you out of Whiskey Run."

The more I say the angrier he gets. He's gripping the rail of the bed like it's a lifeline. Each word he

82

says is deeply enunciated, and his face is red like he's barely keeping it together. "If you believe I would just walk out on you . . . that I would leave—"

I shake my head. I'm completely screwing this up. "No, that's not it at all. It's the opposite. I knew you wouldn't walk away, and I couldn't do that to you. You would have lost everything because of me. But now I have Jessica . . . and it gets worse, Aiden." Tears spring to my eyes. "He found out I was pregnant, and my aunt told me that he planned..." I take a deep breath, finding it hard to even say it out loud. "He planned to take the baby and sell it."

"Over my fuckin' dead body."

I start to cry for real. "Oh Aiden, don't say that."

He grabs on to my hand and threads his fingers with mine. "Gracie, what do you know about me and my family?"

I can feel heat on my cheeks. "I don't know . . . We mostly talked about art. And even then we didn't do a lot of talking."

He laughs. "You're right about that." He strokes his thumb across my wrist. The baby is making little cooing noises, and I pull her in even closer.

"So, my uncle—my mom's brother—is Walker."

My mouth drops. "The Walker?"

He nods. "Yeah, he owns the Whiskey Run Distillery. He actually owns most of Whiskey Run."

"I know Walker. He's the one guy that my father has made sure to steer clear of."

"Well, that was pretty smart at least. But let me tell you, Gracie. With or without my uncle's protection, no one is going to hurt you or Jessica."

---

### Aiden

I PUT my hand around her neck and force her to look at me. "Do you trust me?"

It's the same question I asked her the day we met.

She doesn't hesitate. "I do, Aiden. But I also don't want anything to happen to you."

"Nothing's going to happen to me. I have too much to live for now, Gracie."

She puts her hand on my chest and bunches the shirt in her fingers. "Will you ever forgive me, Aiden?"

I cover her hand with mind and hold it. My heart is racing in my chest because when she left me nine months ago, I never dreamed I would get her back. I had wished and prayed on my knees every day for it, but I was so close to giving up hope.

"I've already forgiven you, Gracie. But you can't ever leave me again." I squeeze her hand tighter. "Promise me. Promise you'll never leave me again."

"I promise."

Before she even gets the words out, I press my lips to hers. With Jessica between us, I'm holding my whole life in my arms. Nothing else matters.

## GRACIE

THEY SAY you should sleep when the baby sleeps, and that's no lie. Besides being exhausted, I'm happy for the first time in a long time.

The doctors came in and said Jessica and I are both doing great, but they are keeping me until tomorrow. Tate and Lakelyn both stopped by when they came to see Violet and Josh Jr. earlier.

I also talked to my Aunt Bethany, and she was so excited about the baby and the fact that Aiden is here with me. Well, he's not with me now.

Now, I'm sitting here in bed with two men staring at me. Aiden had to go take care of some baby plans for the apartment. I assured him I'd be fine by myself, but he wasn't having it.

So, I have the one and only Walker sitting in the corner of my hospital room holding his great niece on his chest.

In the other chair is a brooding friend of Aiden's, Treyton Cree. He's a tattoo artist too.

I cut through the silence. "I feel bad that you both are having to sit with me. I promise I'll be fine. I mean, we're in a hospital. My father won't come here."

Walker smiles. "There's nothing I need to be doing but holding my niece."

I giggle and a snort comes out. "I find that really hard to believe." I mean, he owns more businesses than I can count. I'm sure he should be working.

He laughs. "Okay, I have plenty to do, but nothing is as important as this."

I nod to Treyton. "What about you? You can leave if you want to."

But he's already shaking his head. "I promised Aiden I would stay with you and Jessica. I'm not leaving."

He's gruff. He's been gruff since he got here and Aiden introduced us. Guilt eats at me. I wouldn't like me if I was him either.

In a low soft voice, I tell him, "I didn't want to hurt him."

Treyton's eyes snap to mine, and he sighs loudly. Aiden warned me that Treyton doesn't say much, but it's got me on edge.

"I know you didn't. Aiden explained it to me. I wish that I had done differently. That I had tried to help him find you instead of just thinking the worst of you. That's on me."

The gruff, tattooed guy is not mad. He's eaten up with guilt. "It wasn't your fault—"

But he interrupts me. "Gracie, I tried to get him to forget you. I'm glad he didn't listen."

I don't know what to say. Obviously Treyton has been hurt before. I try and lighten the mood. "That's okay. You can make it up to me by babysitting."

His eyes get big, and he looks over at the sleeping Jessica. I expect him to say no but he surprises me. "If you trust me with her, I'll do it."

I shake my head. "Aiden obviously trusts you, so yeah. I do too."

Treyton nods, and even though he doesn't really smile, his lips do turn up on the sides.

## Aiden

I TAKE the stairs up to the maternity floor. I all but run to get back to Gracie and Jessica. I know they're okay, but I need to make sure I get there first. Uncle Walker's surveillance team already informed me that Mayor Franklin is on the premises. I walk past the two guards outside Gracie's room, and they both nod at me as I walk in.

Gracie's whole face lights up when she sees me. I scan the room and find Jessica lying on my uncle's chest.

"Hey, baby," I say, going to Gracie. She lifts her face, and I can't resist kissing her. Screw it; if Trey and Walker don't like it, they don't have to watch.

Reluctantly, I pull away. I put my hands on Gracie's shoulders. "Gracie, honey, I don't want you to be scared. Your dad is here at the hospital."

She gasps, and her eyes go to Jessica. I put my hand on her arm. "Honey, it's okay. She's safe. You're safe. The only reason I'm telling you is because I need to know if you want to see him. Do you have anything you have to say to him?"

She shakes her head side to side, and it kills me to see how scared she is and to think how many years she put up with his bullshit. "Are you sure? The FBI is here and is waiting on a nod from Uncle Walker. They'll wait if you have something to say to him."

"The FBI?"

I nod. "Yes. I guess your Aunt Bethany had enough dirt on him, and they'd already been investigating him. They tracked him down pretty quickly."

She looks unsure. "So he has done something?"

I squeeze her hand and hesitate. Fuck, I hate having to tell her what a slimeball her dad is.

Uncle Walker clears his throat softly and talks low so as to not wake Jessica. "Yeah, honey, he's responsible for six babies missing and at least seven women. There could be more." Uncle Walker looks at his phone. "He's about to get on the elevator."

"I don't want to see him. I don't want him anywhere near our baby, Aiden."

"Done," Uncle Walker says.

Gracie takes a deep breath and lets it go. "Thank you. Thank all of you."

Uncle Walker gets up and brings the baby to me, putting her in my arms like he's been carrying babies his whole life. He leans over and kisses Gracie on the forehead. "You're family now. You and Jessica. We take care of our own."

Gracie sniffs and puts her arms around Walker's neck. "Thank you, Uncle Walker."

Walker is not really an emotional guy, but he seems affected by her gratitude. His phone dings, and he reads it. "It's done. Mayor Franklin is in custody."

Gracie lies back in the bed, and I swear I can see the relief on her face.

Uncle Walker pats me on the shoulder. "I'm leaving the guards outside until you go home. Take care of your family, son. Call if you need anything."

"Thank you, Walker."

As soon as Walker leaves, Treyton stands up. "I guess that's my cue to go."

"Not so fast, Treyton. I need a hug from you too," Gracie says, holding her arms out toward Trey.

If it was anyone else, I'd probably put a stop to it. But not Trey. He always has my back. But I'm still surprised when he goes to the side of the bed and hugs Gracie.

He pats me on the shoulder and offers a little pat on Jessica's back before he walks out. "Call me if you need anything, brother."

I wait until the door is closed behind him before I turn to Gracie. "Wow! How'd you do that? Trey's not really the huggy type."

She says, "He's been hurt before, hasn't he?"

I nod. "Yeah, pretty bad too."

She cracks a smile. "We'll have to get Violet on it."

"Oh no, Trey would definitely not appreciate being set up. Plus, I'm pretty sure Violet's going to be busy for a while."

She shrugs. "Maybe."

I lay baby Jessica in the bassinet by the bed. With a quick kiss to her forehead, I pull the bed closer so I can sit next to Gracie. "Okay, Momma, what do you need? Are you hungry?"

She shakes her head. "You know what I really want?"

"Whatever you want, it's yours."

"I want you to hold me."

I reach to wrap my arms around her, and she shakes her head and pats the bed. "No, I want to lie in your arms and have you hold me."

I jump up and lower the railing. She moves gingerly to the side, holding a pillow to her stomach.

"Are you hurting?" I ask.

"It's manageable."

I climb into the bed next to her, wrapping my arms around her. She lies against me, her head on my shoulder.

"You okay, honey?"

"As long as I have you and Jessica, I'm happy, Aiden."

"Me too, baby. Me too."

EPILOGUE

GRACIE

## Six Weeks Later

WHO WOULD HAVE THOUGHT at eighteen, I would find my soul mate? And that's the only way I know how to describe Aiden. Everything he does, he does for Jessica and me. When I got home from the hospital, I was surprised to find that in those few hours Aiden was gone from the hospital, he had put together a crib, and I'm pretty sure he bought out the baby store.

Anything Jessica could want or need was set up in the apartment.

And Aiden wasn't lying about our future. We no sooner got out of the hospital than he had a preacher marry us, and even a small reception. Now we're looking at houses.

Our lives have been a whirlwind, but I wouldn't change a thing.

"Gracie, baby, our five o'clock is here."

I smile at my husband and the scantily-clad woman next to him. She's beautiful and can't seem to keep her eyes off my husband, but I can't even be jealous. He only has eyes for me.

"Great, I can work up a design that you'll love. Tell me what you're thinking."

The woman looks at me. "I want him to do it."

Aiden crosses his arms over his chest. He doesn't like anyone to disrespect me. I pat him on the stomach. "He'll be doing the tattoo. But you paid for a Savage Original Artwork. That's me. I'll talk to you, get a feel for what you want, and then draw it. Aiden then guns it."

This was all Aiden's idea. I was hesitant at first, but I'm so glad I did it. I'm able to work and contribute to our family and do it through art.

Even though the woman is reluctant, she finally warms up to me, and I draw her a red rose that she goes crazy over.

"All right, I think Aiden is ready for you."

"Second door on the left. I'll be right there," he tells her.

He waits until the woman walks down the hallway, and he pulls me into his arms. I kiss his lips and smile up at him. "I'm going to get Jessica from the babysitter. We'll be home waiting for you when you're done."

He locks his arms around me and holds me tight just like I like it. "I won't be long."

I trace his nipple through his shirt. "I hope not. You do know Jessica is six weeks old today, and I think it's time we make our marriage official."

He groans into my neck and breathes deeply. "Oh, it's official. There's no doubt you're mine. But yeah, baby. I know what today is. I've been hard thinking about it all day."

My whole body trembles in anticipation. "Well, go hurry. I'll see you at home."

He kisses me deeply and thoroughly, giving me a good indication just how excited and ready he is for tonight. I open my mouth as he groans just as the bells over the door break us apart. A woman walks in, and I pull away but can't help smiling. "Go ahead. I'll help her. See you soon."

He kisses me again before walking off with a wink.

I turn to the woman. "Hi. Can I help you?"

"Yeah, hi. I'm Katie. I have an appointment with Treyton."

I tilt my head. "You look familiar. Do I know you?"

She laughs. "Yeah, I brought you some ice at Jasper Mercy. I'm a nurse. I actually was Violet's nurse. She's the one that convinced me I needed to come to Treyton to get my tattoo."

I giggle almost giddily. "Oh she did, did she?"

Violet is at it again.

Want Treyton and Katie's story?
Pre-Order Torrid now!

# FREE BOOKS

Want FREE BOOKS?

Go to www.authorhopeford.com/freebies

JOIN ME!

## JOIN MY NEWSLETTER & READERS GROUP

www.AuthorHopeFord.com/Subscribe

## JOIN MY READERS GROUP ON FACEBOOK

www.FB.com/groups/hopeford

Find Hope Ford at www.authorhopeford.com

## ABOUT THE AUTHOR

USA Today Bestselling Author Hope Ford writes short, steamy, sweet romances. She loves tattooed, alpha men, instant love stories, and ALWAYS happily ever afters. She has over 100 books and they are all available on Amazon.

To find me on Pinterest, Instagram, Facebook, Goodreads, and more:

www.AuthorHopeFord.com/follow-me

Made in the USA
Columbia, SC
19 July 2024

38889695R00064